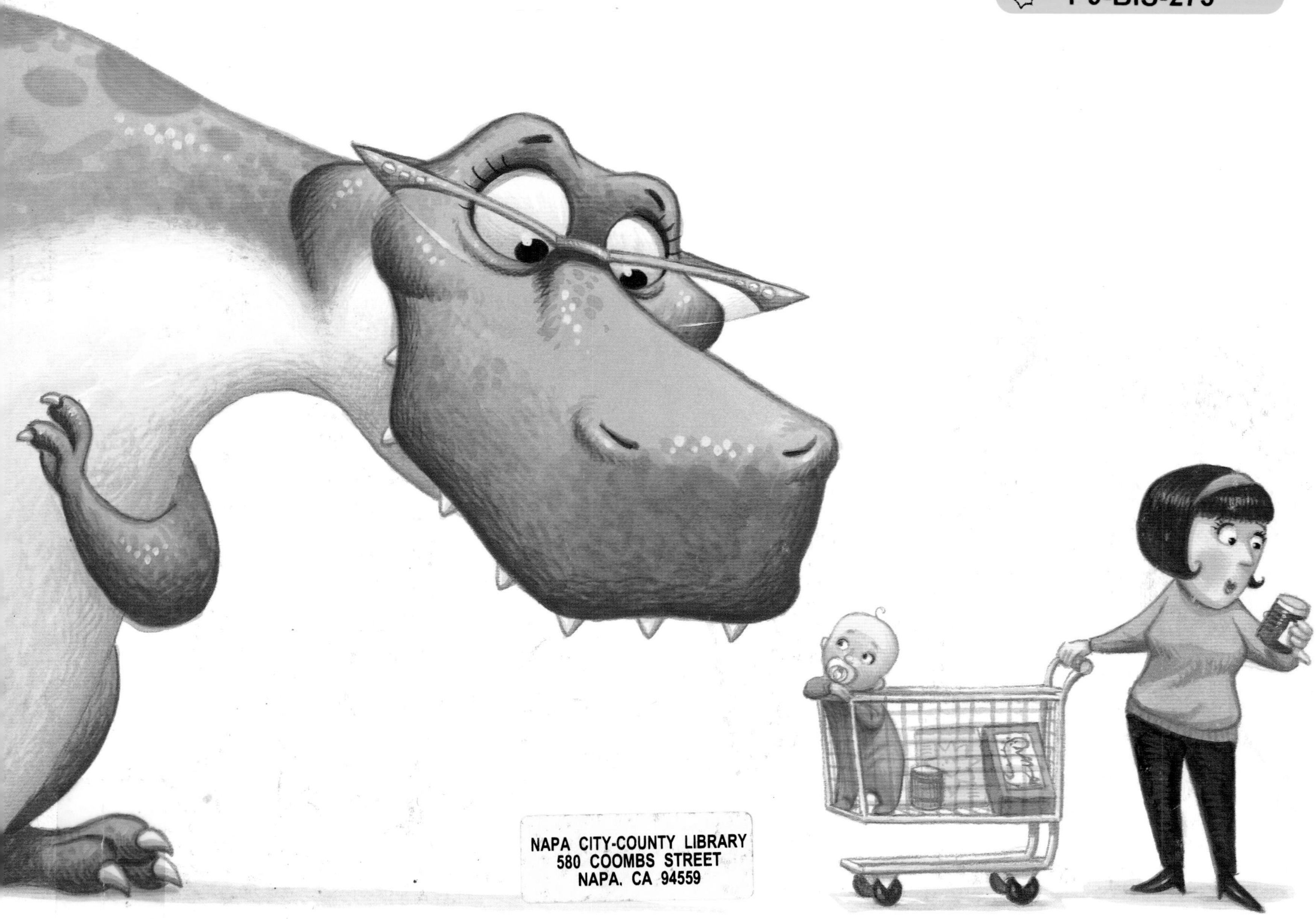

Suppose You Meet a

DiNOSAUR

A First Book of Manners

by JUDY SIERRA
illustrated by TIM BOWERS

ALFRED A. KNOPF
New York

You're shopping at the grocery store.
Surprise!
You see a dinosaur.
This doesn't happen every day.
So, what are you supposed to say?

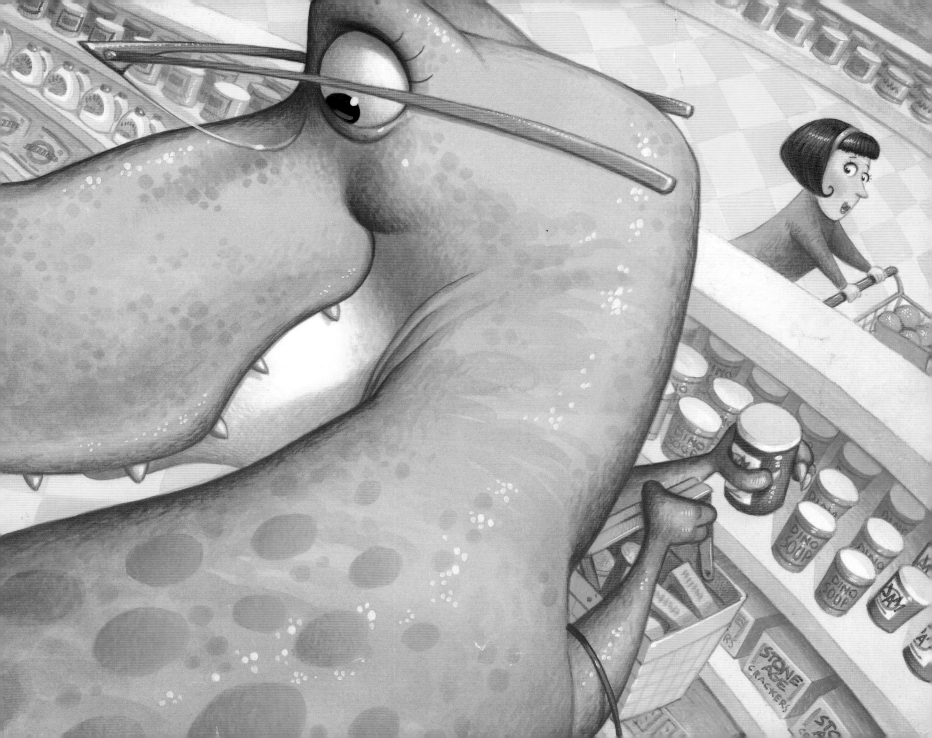

Imagine that the dinosaur
Is standing by a bathroom door.
You have to pee! She's in your way.
Quick! What's the proper thing to say?

Commotion in the produce aisle!
The dinosaur upsets a pile
Of apples, and they roll away.
If you pick them up, what will **she** say?

Your shopping cart begins to spin.
It dings the dino on the shin.
She roars a terrifying roar.
What do you tell the dinosaur?

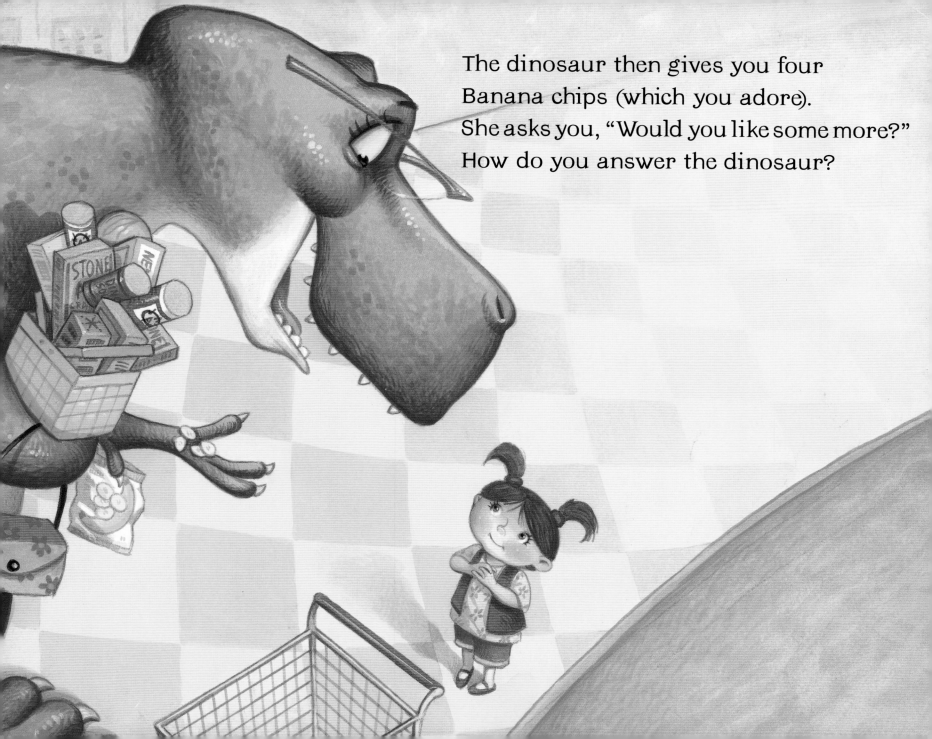

The dinosaur then gives you four
Banana chips (which you adore).
She asks you, "Would you like some more?"
How do you answer the dinosaur?

You want to buy some butter brickle.
Yikes! You need another nickel.
The dinosaur says, "Here's a dime."
What are the magic words this time?

The dinosaur is worried that
A brickle snack would make her fat.
She does not want it, even slightly.
How does she let you know politely?

You find her glasses on the floor
And hand them to the dinosaur.
She smiles and says,
"Why, thank you, dear."
What words does she
    expect to hear?

Out the door of the grocery store
Tromps the friendly dinosaur.
She's waving as she drives away.
I'm sure you know the words to say.

Goodbye.
It was nice to
meet you.

Library of Congress Cataloging-in-Publication Data
Sierra, Judy.
Suppose you meet a dinosaur : a first book of manners / by Judy Sierra ; illustrated by Tim Bowers. — 1st ed.
p. cm.
Summary: Illustrates basic polite behavior that one might need to use while grocery shopping at the same time as a dinosaur.
ISBN 978-0-375-86720-0 (trade) — ISBN 978-0-375-96720-7 (lib. bdg.)
[1. Courtesy—Fiction. 2. Grocery shopping—Fiction. 3. Dinosaurs—Fiction] I. Bowers, Tim, ill. II. Title.
PZ8.3.S577Sup 2011
[E]—dc22
2009037576

The illustrations in this book were created using acrylic paint on bristol board.

MANUFACTURED IN MALAYSIA
January 2012
10 9 8 7 6 5 4 3 2 1

First Edition

Random House Children's Books supports the First Amendment and celebrates the right to read.

FOR JANET SCHULMAN

Suppose you meet an editor
Who mixes words and art.
To make books fun for everyone,
She plays a magic part.

For when you go to turn the page
And then you stop and smile,
You linger and you look again,
As Janet whispers, "Stay awhile."

Thank you, Janet.